Ten-Book Summer

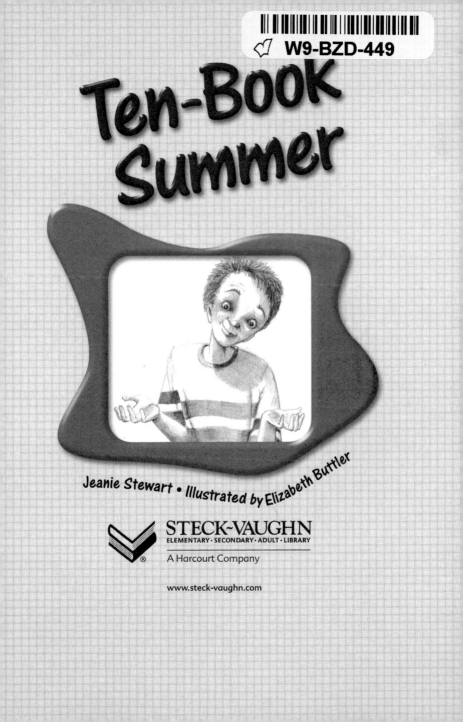

Jeanie Stewart • Illustrated by Elizabeth Buttler

STECK-VAUGHN
ELEMENTARY · SECONDARY · ADULT · LIBRARY

A Harcourt Company

www.steck-vaughn.com

ISBN 0-7398-5106-3

Printed in the United States of America.

1 2 3 4 5 6 7 8 9 LB 06 05 04 03 02

Contents

Chapter One

Party Summer

This was it, day one of Party Summer. It was my first summer as a teenager. School was out, and I was 13. Things were going to be different.

This wasn't going to be a little-kid summer of hanging around the apartment. This summer was going to be hot sun, cold water, and teenaged girls. My best friend, Bud, and I planned to hang out at the Sun Fun Pool every day.

I finished my cereal as quickly as I could. The sooner we got to the pool, the sooner the amusement could begin.

"Korbett!" Dad yelled from the living room. "We need to talk."

That was a bad sign. Everyone calls me Koby. Nobody calls me Korbett unless I'm in trouble.

Dad came into the kitchen. "Your mom and I are upset about your grades," he said.

It was summer. Why worry about grades now?

"Everybody's grades dropped last year," I said. "Middle school is hard."

"How many times have I told you that grades are important?" he asked.

He'd told me a million times, and I didn't want to hear it again.

"You're right, Dad," I said. "I'll try harder." I eased toward the door.

"Not so fast, son," he said. "Your teacher says that you don't work up to your potential. That means you can do the work, but you don't. You're lazy."

"Okay," I said. "But could we talk about this later? Bud's expecting me."

Dad glared. "I'll come right to the point. Your mother thinks you should read five books as a summer project."

"Five books!" I howled.

"But now I think that isn't such a good idea," he added.

"Whew! Thanks, Dad." I grabbed the doorknob.

He raised his voice to stop me. "I think ten books would be better."

"No fair!" I cried.

"And I want a written report on each," he said.

"Nobody does book reports in the summer," I complained.

"You will. Ten of them," Dad assured me. He walked off without another word.

Ten books were more than I had read in my whole life. The thought of all those words worried me, but I couldn't let this get me down. I'd just have to figure a way out of it later.

Rushing out the apartment door, I ran right into my neighbor, Nina Song. Nina is my age and has had a crush on me forever.

"What are you doing here?" I asked. "I thought you were spending the summer with your mom in Miami."

"No," she said. "Dad wants me to stay with him."

Right. I think she wanted to stay here just to annoy me.

"Where are we going?" she asked, falling into step beside me.

"WE aren't going anywhere," I corrected her. "I'M going to Bud's. And I'm late!"

I ran for the stairs. I know it was mean of me. Nina couldn't keep up with me there.

In five minutes I was at Bud's door two floors down.

"Hurry!" I said. "Let's get to the pool before something else goes wrong."

"I can't go, man." Bud calls everyone *man*.

"But we have plans," I reminded him.

"So does my mom," he answered. "Her plans are for me to stay home with my little sister."

"You're spoiling Party Summer," I whined.

Bud shrugged. "I can't help it, man. Mom says she's not paying a baby-sitter to watch Katy when I can do it. Mothers can be such pains."

"Fathers, too," I said. I told him about my dad's ten-book plan.

6

"Oh, that's not so bad. Book reports are easy," Bud said. "All you have to do is copy that stuff from the back of the book."

Bud looked in his desk, on a bookcase or two, and finally under his bed. He found one of his old reports and gave it to me.

"Thanks," I said. I stuck the paper into my pocket. At least one of my problems was solved.

Chapter Two

Lessons Learned

"Did you think I couldn't tell it was copied from the back of a book?" Mom yelled. She'd been yelling at me ever since I'd given her my first report. "I can't believe you'd try something so dishonest!"

She opened the front door and motioned me into the hall. "I hope you've learned something from our little talk this morning."

Oh, yes, I'd learned three things.

One, never use your best friend's book report if it has a big red *D-* at the top. Two, if you're going to copy from the back of a book, change a few words. Three, don't expect a mother to understand when you tell her that the library is not where a boy wants to be seen in the summer.

"Go straight to the library and start a real report!" She slammed the apartment door behind me.

"I'm going," I said to the closed door. I just hoped I could get there, grab a book, and get out without anyone I knew seeing me.

I guess being invisible was too much to ask. I was hardly inside the library when Mario Mendoza greeted me with a whack on my back. He's the most popular guy in our class. What was he doing at the library?

"I brought my little brother to story hour," he said. "Are you here for story hour, too, Koby? Aren't you too tall for those little chairs?"

He whacked my arm and laughed at his own joke. I didn't think it was that funny.

I stepped away and rubbed my arm. "I'm picking up a book for my mom," I said. Well, it was true, in a way.

Mario said, "When you're done here, you should come over to the Sun Fun Pool. A bunch of us will be there all day."

After a goodbye whack on the back, he left me alone in the land of too many books.

A moment later, someone bumped my knees from behind. "Guess who?" a voice said.

I didn't have to guess. It was Nina the pest.

"I saw you with Mario," she said. "What was his big rush?"

"Who knows? Maybe he's got a life," I grumbled.

"Your mom told me you might need help finding a book," she said.

I couldn't believe my mom had told Nina. I shook my head. "No, I don't need any help."

As usual, Nina didn't listen to me. "This one is good. It's about a boy who wants to play baseball," she said. She pulled a fat book off the shelf and dropped it into my arms. It weighed a ton.

"No, thanks," I said, putting it back. "That's not what I'm looking for."

"No? I thought you liked sports."

We walked across the aisle. She grabbed another book, even bigger than the last.

"Here's a good one," she said. "It's about a boy in love with the girl next door."

I nearly choked. "That's definitely not what I want," I said.

"Well, help me out here. What do you want?" she asked.

Suddenly, I saw exactly what I wanted, but it had nothing to do with books. The most beautiful girl I'd ever seen was standing beside the magazine rack. She smiled at me.

Nina tapped my arm. "Koby, are you listening to me?"

Clearly, I wasn't.

"Don't you want a book?" she asked.

No. I didn't. I also didn't want to be standing so close to Nina. If my dream girl saw us together, she might get the wrong idea. I stepped away.

"Koby, focus! You're here to get a book," Nina said. She was starting to make me really angry.

"Did my mom send you here to nag me?" I asked her.

"No, I'm just trying to help," she answered. "Do you like books about animals?"

"No," I said.

"Cars?"

"No."

"Outer space?"

"NO!"

"Well, Koby, I give up," she said. "What kind of books are you looking for?"

"Short ones!" I yelled.

A librarian gave us a dirty look. "Quiet," he scolded.

Nina changed her voice to a whisper. "Okay. Short books. Let's look over here."

I ignored Nina. I was too busy watching my dream girl. Even the way she flipped the pages of her magazine was cute.

All at once, she looked up and caught me staring. I was embarrassed, but she didn't seem to be. She grinned and waved at me. I tried to wave back, but couldn't. I froze. My arms felt heavier than Nina's books. ⚡

My dream girl shrugged, dropped her magazine back into the rack, and turned to go.

"Hurry, look!" I grabbed Nina and spun her around. "Do you know that girl?"

Nina sighed and rolled her eyes. "I met her last week. Her name is Rowena. She just moved here."

Rowena. Even her name was beautiful. I stood on tiptoe to keep her in sight as long as I could.

Nina poked me. "Here's an easy book," she said.

I pretended not to hear her.

"It's about a dog that gets stolen from his home," she said more loudly. "I read it ages ago, but I can still remember everything that happened. It's good. You should read it."

Suddenly a brilliant idea came to me. Why should I read the book if Nina already had? If I could get her to tell me enough about it, I could write a report without reading a word.

"Hmm, that sounds interesting," I said. "Tell me more."

So she did.

"That's the book for me," I said when she'd finished.

Nina offered to walk back home with me, but I said no. I was in a hurry. I had to write down everything she'd said about the dog book before I forgot. This was going to be one great report! Not one word would be copied from the back of the book.

Chapter Three

Back in the Library

"Back in the library so soon, Koby?" Nina the shadow asked me the next day.

"Yes, thanks to you, I am," I grumbled.

"I came over this morning to see if they had any new romance books," she said.

Sure she had. My mother had probably sent her to spy on me.

I dropped the dog book on the table in front of her. "Why didn't you tell me that the dog died at the end of this dumb book?"

"I didn't want to spoil it for you," she said.

"Well, you did spoil it," I snapped. "My mom was furious."

Nina wrinkled her forehead. "You aren't making sense. Why would your mom be mad about a dog dying in a book?"

I told Nina about my ten-book summer project and how I'd done a report on the dog book.

"I didn't have time to really read it," I said. "So I just wrote down the things you told me."

She frowned. "That's not the same as a book report."

"Maybe not, but it was working just fine until my mom started asking questions. If you had told me the right stuff, I could have answered them," I told her.

I thought Nina would take my side, since she was so crazy about me. She didn't.

"No wonder your mom was mad," she said. "You tried to trick her."

"Mom was the one with the tricks," I objected. "How was I supposed to know she'd read the book?"

"Koby, you were cheating!"

"It's just a silly book report." I didn't want to talk about it anymore. "Just leave me alone," I said. I stomped away.

I was leaning against a shelf, feeling sorry for myself, when Mario walked up.

"Hi, Koby," he said.

I dodged before he could whack me on the back.

"Are you here getting more books for your mother?" he asked.

"I guess you could say that," I said. "Are you dropping off your little brother again?"

"No. Today I'm picking up a movie for my mom."

Movie? Why hadn't anyone told me that the library had movies?

"You mean you can check out movies the same way you check out a book?" I asked. I couldn't believe it. Maybe the library wasn't such a bad place after all.

"Sure. I do it all the time," he answered. As if to prove how easy it was, he grabbed *Romeo and Juliet* and left.

I pumped one arm into the air and did a little victory dance. This was the perfect answer to my book report problem. All I had to do was pick a movie that was also a book.

But how could I get it past Mom? She was smart. The minute I popped the movie into the player, she would know what I was up to. I had to think of a way to work this.

Nina was the answer! It didn't take me long to find her.

"I'm sorry I was so rude earlier," I said. "I shouldn't have yelled at you. Can I make it up to you with a movie?"

Nina's eyes got really big. "Are you asking me to go to a movie?"

"Well, not exactly," I said. "I thought maybe we could get a movie from the library and watch it at your apartment."

Nina liked the idea. She helped me pick out the perfect movie in no time. We were on our way out when I saw Rowena again. I stopped so fast that Nina and I nearly tripped over each other.

"I need to check out one more thing," I told Nina. "You go ahead. I'll meet you outside."

After Nina left, Rowena smiled and waved at me. I waved back. At least my arms were working today. She motioned for me to come over. This was too good to be true.

I pointed to myself and said, "Who, me?"

She nodded.

My feet felt like they had been glued to the floor, but somehow I walked over to her.

"I'm Rowena Flores," she said. "I saw you earlier, talking to Mario Mendoza."

She had noticed me! I hadn't imagined it after all. My voice squeaked as I introduced myself.

"Are you and Mario good friends?" she asked.

"Oh sure, Mario is a great guy," I said. "He's friends with everybody."

"Is that your girlfriend?" she asked.

I looked in the direction she was pointing and saw Nina's face pressed against the glass door.

"That's Nina," I said.

Rowena stepped closer to me. Her hair smelled like oranges, berries, and lemons all mixed together. My heart pounded. I started to sweat. I had to hurry and ask her the big question before I backed out.

"My best friend and I are going to watch a movie at Nina's tonight. Would you like to join us?" I held my breath waiting for her answer.

Rowena pushed her hair away from her face. She tapped her finger against her cheek. She was taking much too long.

I closed my eyes. She was going to reject me, and I'd be crushed.

"I love movies," she said at last. "What time should I be there?"

Were my ears working? Had she really said yes? More importantly, would she really show up?

Chapter Four

The Big Date

I thought 6:30 would never arrive, but finally it did. I rushed over to Nina's.

"Come in, Koby," Nina said, opening the door. "You look nice."

"Thanks," I said. She looked nice, too, but I didn't say so. I didn't want her to get the wrong idea.

She led me over to the couch and sat down. It looked a little too cozy for me, so I sat in a chair. My stomach rumbled.

"Are you hungry?" she asked.

I could feel my face turning red. "Yes," I
said. Actually, my stomach makes funny noises
when I get nervous, but just try explaining
that to people. It was easier to let Nina think
I was hungry.

"You're in luck. Dad is making us a pizza." She slid a bowl of chips down the table. "You can snack on these while we wait."

I grabbed a chip but didn't eat it. I didn't want to have chip breath when Rowena got here. The phone rang, and I jumped. The chip crumbled in my hand.

"Nina," Mr. Song called from the kitchen. "The phone is for you."

Nina handed me a napkin and went to the phone. When she returned, she plopped down on the couch and glared at me.

"That was Bud on the phone," she said.

I knew I had some quick explaining to do, but about that time, Mr. Song brought in the pizza.

"Mmm, that smells great," I said. He and I said a few polite words to each other, but I could hardly pay attention. Nina's stare was making me more nervous by the second.

She didn't say anything until her dad returned to the kitchen. Then she let me have it.

"Okay, Koby. What's going on?" she asked. "Bud said to tell you that his mom is working late. He has to baby-sit and can't come."

I blushed. "I guess I forgot to tell you that I invited Bud."

"I guess you did," she said.

I stuck my hands in my pockets and sunk lower in the chair. "I didn't think you'd mind."

The doorbell rang.

"Wait, Nina," I said, scrambling to my feet. "Before you answer that, there's something else you should know." I cleared my throat. "I also invited Rowena. Remember her? She's that new girl from the library."

The doorbell rang again, but Nina didn't move. She just sat there looking up at me with big, puppy-dog eyes.

"I was only trying to be nice," I said. "You know how hard it is to meet people when you're the new kid in town."

"You could have told me, Koby."

"I was going to tell you on the way home from the library. Really I was, but you were talking, and it seemed rude to interrupt."

I could tell she didn't believe me. "Are you mad?" I asked.

"No," she said quietly.

The doorbell rang a third time. Nina stood with a sigh. "I guess Dad should have made a bigger pizza."

One thing I can say about Nina is that she's a good sport. She smiled sweetly, opened the door, and invited Rowena in.

Rowena stepped around Nina and walked right over to me.

"I hope I'm not early," she said. "Where's your friend? He is coming, isn't he?"

I couldn't speak. All I could do was stare at her beautiful face.

Nina answered for me. "Bud can't come."

Rowena raised one eyebrow. "Who's Bud?" she asked me.

My mouth opened, but no sound came out.

"Bud is Koby's best friend," Nina answered. I was beginning to feel like a ventriloquist's dummy.

Rowena frowned at me. "But I saw you with Mario at the library. I thought he was your best friend."

When I didn't answer, she looked from me to Nina. Nina said nothing, so Rowena turned back to me.

"Ro—" My voice squeaked halfway through her name. I tried to swallow, but my mouth was completely dry.

Rowena yanked up her sleeve and looked at her watch.

"Oh, I just remembered something I have to do," she said. "It's really important. I'd like to stay, but I can't." She backed toward the door. "I'll see you guys around."

She pivoted on her heels and was out the door before I could say a single word.

Nina closed the door. "Sorry, Koby."

"She only came because she was hoping to meet Mario Mendoza," I mumbled. "She was just using me."

Nina nodded. "There seems to be a lot of that going around lately."

"What did you say?" I asked.

"Never mind," she said. "Forget about Rowena. Let's watch the movie." She picked up the remote control and turned on the TV and VCR. "Look on the bright side. At least there's plenty of pizza for two."

We ate the whole thing without any trouble.

It was actually fun watching the movie with Nina. We laughed and said silly things about the actors. Before long, I forgot to be miserable.

We talked so much that I stayed even after the movie ended. When Nina wasn't nagging me about doing the right thing, she was really easy to talk to.

As it turned out, I wasn't the only one having a bad-luck summer. Nina's mother had a new job and she was traveling a lot.

Although Nina was happy about her mother's promotion, she was disappointed that they couldn't spend the summer together. I guess I wasn't the reason she was sticking around here after all.

It was late when Nina walked me to the door.

"I'm glad you were able to come over, Koby," she said. "As mad as your mom has been, I'm surprised she let you leave your room."

"She wasn't wild about the idea," I said. "But when I told her I was coming over to work on my report, she said okay."

Nina shook her head at me like I was hopeless. "You really shouldn't lie to your mom, you know."

"I didn't," I said.

Suddenly Nina groaned as if she'd eaten too much pizza.

"Oh, no," she said. "You aren't planning to write a book report about this movie, are you?"

"Sure, why not?" I said. "It was a book before it was a movie, wasn't it?"

"It was, but trust me, Koby, it's not a good idea." ⚡

I opened the door. I could tell she had more to say, but I didn't want to hear it.

"Nina, I've had fun tonight," I said. "Don't spoil it by giving me the dishonesty talk again."

She didn't, but the look on her face made me feel really bad.

Chapter Five

Starting Over

I was eating breakfast the next morning when Nina knocked on the door.

"Koby, have you written that report yet?" she asked as I let her in.

"No—"

She cut me off by putting her hand over my mouth. "Good, because I need to tell you something before you write it." She sat down at the kitchen table. "I should have told you last night, but I couldn't. I was too upset that you were going to fake another book report."

"It's okay, Nina. You can quit worrying,"
I said, sitting across from her. "I'm not going
to write a report from the movie."

She let out a loud breath. "You're not?"

"No," I said. "I'm really not." I scooted the
milk and cereal in her direction. "Have some
breakfast, and I'll explain."

When I was sure her mouth was too full for her to interrupt me, I began. "Last night when I got home, I was so busy feeling sorry for myself, I couldn't sleep. I kept thinking about Rowena. I couldn't understand how she could be so mean. The more I thought about how she had used me to meet Mario, the madder I got.

"Then it hit me. I did the same thing to you, twice. I used you to get my book reports done. I feel awful. I was wrong, and I'm sorry. Anyway, I've learned my lesson. I'm through being dishonest, even on those silly book reports. So you don't have to lecture."

"I didn't come over here to lecture," she answered.

"Then what did you want to tell me?" I asked.

She wiped a drop of milk off her chin. "It doesn't matter now."

I leaned over, almost in her face. "Come on, Nina, tell me anyway. I want to know."

"Well, remember that girl in the movie who had the pet monkey?" she asked.

"Of course," I said. "She was the main character."

"In the book, the main character was a boy, and he had a pet dog."

"You're kidding!" I said, amazed. "Can you imagine how mad my mom would have been if I had handed her a report about a girl with a monkey?"

"I'm glad we don't have to find out," she said.

"You and me both! Why would movie makers change stuff like that?"

Nina shrugged. "I don't know. Maybe monkeys are easier to work with."

"Or maybe the director had a daughter who wanted to be a movie star," I said.

"No," she said with a grin. "I'll bet the director had a pet monkey who wanted to be a star."

I waved my hands. "No. No! I know the real reason the movie makers change things from the book version. They want to trap poor middle-school kids who try to fake their book reports."

Nina put her hand over her mouth and started to giggle. I laughed too. I couldn't help it. I felt so relieved that she wasn't mad at me.

"So what are you going to do about a report?" Nina asked.

"What else? Read a book, I guess."

"And then read nine more?" she asked.

I sighed. "Let's take this one baby step at a time." I carried our bowls to the sink. "Would you come to the library and help me find a book?"

"Sure," she said. "When do you want to go?"

"We'll go later this afternoon, okay? Bud doesn't have to baby-sit this morning. He and I are going to the Sun Fun Pool.

"That sounds like fun," she said.

"Hey, why don't you come with us?"

Why hadn't I ever noticed what a pretty smile Nina had? I had a feeling there was hope for Party Summer after all.